Playtime with Monster

www.fatmoonbooks.com

ISBN-10: 1481260537

ISBN-13: 978-1481260534

Printed in the United States of America.

This book belongs to

_____

Bedtime was never fun for Eric. He hated washing up. He hated brushing his teeth. And he hated putting on his pajamas. Eric would rather play games than get ready for bed. That's when Eric's mom decided to tell him about the monster.

"**W**hat monster, Mommy?" Eric asked excitedly, jumping up and down. He loved dinosaurs and dragons and animals of every kind.

"I'm talking about the monster that'll come and play with you," replied Mom. "I'll tell you all about it and what to do after you're all washed up and ready for bed."

So for the very first time, in all of Eric's four long years of life, he willingly took his bath, brushed his teeth, and put on his pajamas. Eric proudly smiled and declared, "I'm ready!"

"Wow, that was super, honey," Mom cheerfully beamed back. "Now I'll tell you what to do. First we'll head to the kitchen."

"But I don't want a snack. I want to hear about the monster!" Eric protested.

Mom grabbed Eric's hand and told him, "You may not want a snack, but I know someone else who would love a snack." Eric looked up into mom's face and she grinned and winked at him.

"Oh! The monster!!!" Eric exclaimed.

Eric and mom filled a plate with chocolate chip cookies, returned to his bedroom and placed it next to his bed.

Then mom said, "Now, you need to get under your covers, and say, 'Monster, monster, one, two, three...won't you come out and play with me? This monster will do anything for food, especially cookies."

"I got it," said Eric. He leapt into his bed and pulled the covers over himself. Then he repeated what his mom told him to say after she left.

"Monster, monster, one, two, three...won't you come out and play with me? ...And I have cookies for you!!!"

Eric heard someone stomping around his room. Was it the monster?

"Mmm, yummy cookies!" someone cried.

Eric took a peek from under his covers and saw ...the monster!

"Ooh!" said Eric. "It worked. Are you here to play with me?"

"Grrr...," said the monster. "What do you want to play?"

"Let's play horsey. Give me a ride around the room, please, Mr. Monster."

The monster came up next to the bed, got down on his four paws, and Eric climbed on top of him, grabbing onto a handful of fur. "Hang on now," the monster growled at him. They galloped all around the room many times with Eric giggling and bouncing up and down.

Finally, the monster came to a halt and placed Eric back onto his bed. "Good night now, little boy, and thank you for the cookies," said the monster.

"Thank you for playing with me," said Eric. "Will you come back tomorrow? I'll put out some more treats for you."

The monster didn't say anything, but walked towards the door, stopped before leaving and smiled at Eric.

The next night, Eric zoomed to the bathroom. He washed up and brushed his teeth, and then hurried to put on his pajamas.

Afterwards, he rushed off to the kitchen and said to his mom, "Look, Mommy! I'm all done. Now can I please have some cookies to give to the monster?"

His mom studied him closely.

"Did you brush your teeth?" she asked.

"Yes! My breath is nice and minty," Eric said.

"Alright, then you can have some cookies for the monster," his mom said.

They carried the cookies to the room, and Eric scurried under his covers. Eric's mom left the room.

"Monster, monster, one, two, three...won't you come out and play with me? ...And I have cookies for you!!!"

Once again Eric heard a stomping sound. There were loud crunching noises as the monster snacked on the cookies.

"Yum, yum! Chocolate chip, my favorite!" said the monster.

ic hopped out of bed.

"Mr. Monster! You're back. Will you play with me?" asked Eric eagerly, before remembering his manners. "Please?"

"Hmmm, since these were good cookies...sure! What do you want to play?" The monster waited for Eric's reply.

"How about hide and go seek?" Eric said.

"Okay," said the monster, covering his eyes. "One, two, three..."

"Wait! I'm not ready," Eric giggled.

Eric hid under his bed. The monster found him. Then the monster hid in the laundry basket. Eric found him, too. They played for a while, before the monster said, "It's time for bed. Goodnight, little boy, and thank you for the cookies."

"Thank you for playing with me," said Eric with a yawn. The monster tucked Eric into bed and left.

"The monster's visits continued, and Eric became very quick at washing up, brushing his teeth, and putting on his pajamas. He became so quick that his mom had to send him back to the bathroom because he still had soap bubbles in his hair.

One night, Eric went to the kitchen and asked for some more cookies to give to the monster.

"I'm sorry, Eric. We don't have any more cookies. I'll make more tomorrow," said his mom.

"What?! But I wanted to play with the monster!" exclaimed Eric.

"Well, here are some apples. You can give these to the monster," his mom told him. "Besides, apples are healthier, and I happen to know that the monster loves them."

"Okay," said Eric.

Eric went to bed and snuggled under the blankets.

"Monster, monster, one, two, three...won't you come out and play with me!" Eric shouted, before adding, "I don't have any cookies, but I do have some nice apples."

Eric waited. Then there was the familiar stomping noise and the munching of apples.

Eric pulled off the covers and grinned at the monster.

"Yay, Mr. Monster! Let's play," said Eric.

The monster swallowed a bite of apple. "And what shall we play tonight?" he asked.

"Helicopter!" cried Eric, stretching his arms straight up. "Let's play helicopter, pleeease!"

The monster picked Eric up by his arms and began to turn on the spot. They spun round and round. Eric let out a squeal as his feet were lifted off the ground.

"Wheeee!" said Eric.

They did this several times, before the monster's arms got tired and he plopped Eric down on the bed.

"Whew! Good night, little boy, and thank you for the apples," said the monster.

"Goodnight and thank you for playing, Dad— I mean, Mr. Monster!" Eric hurried to correct himself. He looked shamefully at the monster for having accidentally broken the game.

But, Eric's dad just smiled, kissed his son on the top of his head, and said, "Sleep tight, son. And don't worry; I'm sure Mr. Monster will be back tomorrow, especially since Mommy is making a big batch of chocolate chip cookies!"